Squirrel's Treasure Hunt

By Annie Cobb • Illustrated by Kathy Wilburn

Silver Press

Produced by Chardiet Unlimited, Inc. and Daniel Weiss Associates, Inc.
33 West 17th Street, New York, NY 10011

Copyright © 1991 Daniel Weiss Associates, Inc./
Chardiet Unlimited, Inc.

Illustration copyright by Kathy Wilburn

Educational Consultant:
Dr. Priscilla Lynch

GOING PLACES™ is a trademark of Daniel Weiss Associates, Inc.
and Chardiet Unlimited, Inc.

Published by Silver Press, a division of
Silver Burdett Press, Inc., Simon & Schuster, Inc.
Prentice Hall Bldg., Englewood Cliffs, NJ 07632
For information address: Silver Press.

Printed in the United States of America
10 9 8 7 6 5 4 3 2 1

Library of Congress Cataloging-in-Publication Data

Cobb, Annie
Squirrel's Treasure Hunt/written by Annie Cobb;
illustrated by Kathy Wilburn
p.   cm.—(Going places)
Summary: Squirrel and Raccoon get lost on a treasure hunt until a
bird helps them learn the four directions.
1.Going—Juvenile literature. [1.Going] I. Wilburn, Kathy, ill. II.
Title. III. Series: Going places
(Englewood Cliffs, N.J.)

ISBN 0-671-70391-9 (LSB)

ISBN 0-671-70395-1

Early one morning Squirrel knocked on Raccoon's door. "Wake up!" he called. "Look what I found."

Raccoon pulled the covers over his head. "Go away! I want to sleep!" he said. But Squirrel knocked even harder.

Sleepy Raccoon opened the door. Squirrel came in waving a piece of paper. "Look!" he said.

Raccoon read:

GO ON A TREASURE HUNT
START AT OWL'S HOUSE

"Let's start right now," Squirrel yelled.

"Oh, all right!" yawned Raccoon. "I'll help you find the treasure. But then I'm going back to sleep."

So Squirrel and Raccoon ran through the woods to Owl's house.

"I don't see any treasure," Raccoon said.

"It's a treasure *hunt*," Squirrel explained. "That means we have to look for clues. Look, I see one there!" He pointed to a piece of paper hanging from a branch. The paper said:

GO EAST UNTIL YOU COME TO A BIG ROCK

"Which way is East?" said Raccoon.

"Maybe it's ahead of us," Squirrel said.

"Or behind us," said Raccoon.

"Maybe it's to the left," said Squirrel.

"Or to the right," said Raccoon.

"Oh dear," said Squirrel. "I'm getting all mixed up."

"Quiet down there!" came a voice. It was Owl. "I'm trying to sleep. Can't you see the sun is up? That's when owls go to bed!"

"Sorry," Squirrel said. "We were just trying to decide which way is East."

Owl said, "East is where the sun comes up every morning. And when the sun comes up...Z-Z-Z-Z." Owl fell fast asleep.

Squirrel and Raccoon turned toward the morning sun. They kept walking East until they came to a great big rock. A piece of paper was stuck to the rock. The paper said:

TURN RIGHT TO BEAVER'S POND
AND TAKE BEAVER'S FERRY

"Follow me," Squirrel said. "I think I know the way!" And he pointed to his right.

"So do I," said Raccoon, and *he* pointed to *his right*.

"Where *are* you going, Raccoon?" Squirrel yelled. "Something is wrong."

"Yes, indeed!" came a voice. Mrs. Rabbit came out of her burrow. "Something is *very* wrong," she said. "You're stomping on my roof."

"Sorry," said Squirrel. "Raccoon and I have a problem. Both of us are going *right*, but we are going in *opposite* directions. How can that be?"

"That's because you are facing in opposite directions!" sighed Mrs. Rabbit. "Try facing the same way. And *please* try not to *stomp*," she added. "My bunnies are still asleep."

So Squirrel and Raccoon both faced the big rock. Then they both turned right and walked to Beaver's Pond.

Beaver's ferry was just pulling out. "Wait!" Squirrel called. And he and Raccoon hopped aboard.

The ride was lots of fun. Beaver told funny jokes. Bear did a little dance. Even the cat, who hated water, joined in when Raccoon sang a sailing song.

Soon they reached the shore. Another piece of
paper was hanging from a willow tree. It said:

GO SOUTH TO BLUEBERRY HILL

"Another clue!" grumbled Raccoon. "This treasure
is very hard to find! Which way is South?"

"Maybe I can help," said Bear. "I'm going to Blueberry Hill to pick berries. My mother told me just to follow my nose."

So Squirrel, Raccoon, and Bear stuck out their noses and followed them—right into the woods. Soon all the trees began to look alike. They walked and walked.

"I don't think your nose knows the way, Bear," Raccoon grumbled.

"I think we're lost," said Squirrel.

"I know the way," said a little bird. "In the spring birds fly North. In the fall we fly South. I'll help you find Blueberry Hill in no time."

Bird drew a big circle in the dirt.

"The world is round like this circle," Bird said. "These are the four directions. North is at the North Pole. South is at the South Pole. North and South are opposite each other. And here are East and West. East and West are opposites, too."

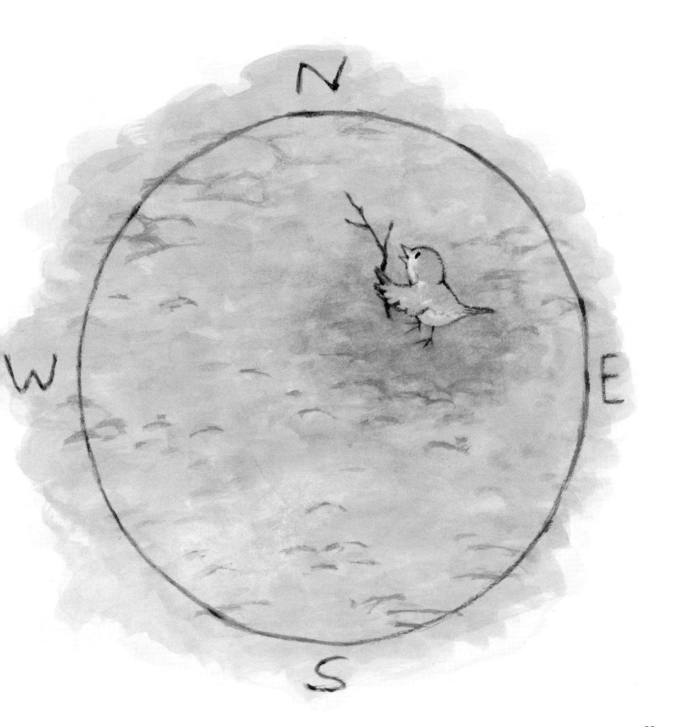

21

"This is making me dizzy," said Raccoon.

"I think I get it," Squirrel said. "I'm facing West, so East is behind me and South is to my left."

"I get it, too," said Bear. "I am facing East, so West is behind me and South is to my right."

"Yes," Bird said.

"North, South, East, and West.
If you know *one* direction
You know the rest."

So the four friends went South to Blueberry Hill. There they found a big bag full of cookies. A piece of paper was tied to the bag. It said:

PICK SOME BERRIES AND STOP FOR A SNACK
THEN LOOK AT THE COOKIES TO FIND YOUR WAY BACK

"At last I know how to follow some of the directions," sighed Raccoon.

Then the friends picked blueberries, played games, and ate many cookies.

Near the bottom of the cookie bag there was another message. It said:

GO BACK THE WAY YOU CAME AND
STOP AT THE HOUSE WITH THE GREEN SHUTTERS

It was getting late. Bear and Bird said goodbye.

Squirrel was staring at the cookies. "Raccoon," he said. "The cookie is a circle just like the one Bird made. Look, it says N S E W—North, South, East, West. We can use the cookie to find our way back."

Raccoon and Squirrel knew that they were in the South. So they turned around and went in the opposite direction. They went North back to Beaver's ferry.

And North and West back across Beaver Pond.

And North to the big rock.

And West to Owl's tree.

From there they started walking toward Raccoon's house. But along the way, guess what Squirrel saw? A little house with shutters of green!

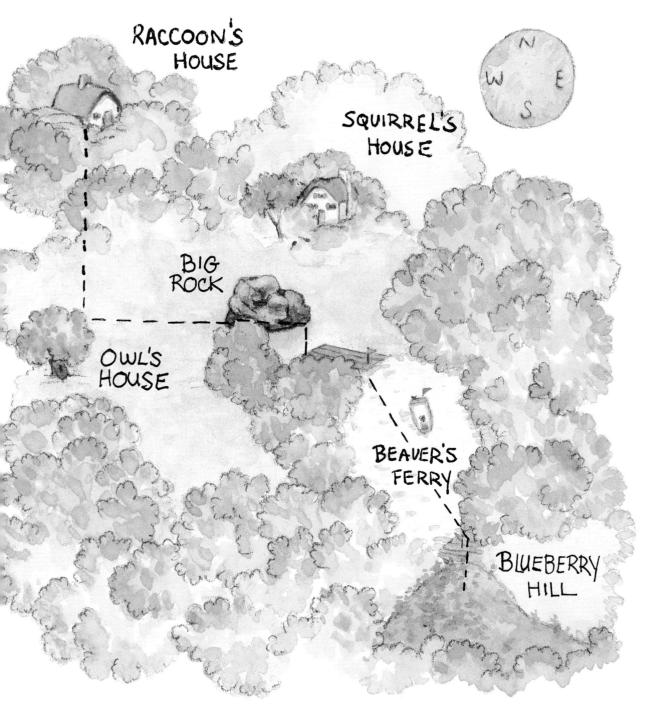

RACCOON'S HOUSE

SQUIRREL'S HOUSE

N
W E
S

BIG ROCK

OWL'S HOUSE

BEAVER'S FERRY

BLUEBERRY HILL

29

"Hey!" he shouted. "That looks just like *my* house! It *is* my house! And there's Grandpa at the door."

"Hello," said Grandpa. "I knew you'd find it."

"Find what?" said Raccoon.

"The treasure," said Grandpa. He gave Raccoon and Squirrel two shovels and said:

> "Walk twenty steps
> To the old birch tree
> And that is where
> The treasure will be."

So Squirrel and Raccoon dug a hole beneath the
birch tree. Sure enough, they found a great big sack.
It was filled with nuts and seeds and berries—
the perfect treasure for a wonderful animal supper.

They ate and ate, and there was still enough left over
to share with all of their friends.